A Max & Colby Adv

Who is UP in OL ree?

Janis Hennessey

Illustrated by Teresa Street

ISBN:1508731128
ISBN:9781508731122

To Karen, Bill, Jody - jh
To Jessica - ts

Max and Colby are very curious dogs. They are especially curious about the strange animal up in their big tree.

Friendship - Fiction, Animals -dogs, Ages: 2-7, Reading level - First grade

Big Tree Press
55 Applevale Drive
Dover, NH 03820
USA

Table of Contents

"Who is Up in *OUR* Tree?" is the fourth of the Max & Colby Adventures.
We welcome you to check out the other stories at
Amazon.com & **Kindle.com**

English:	French:
Zooming Fun	A toute vitesse
A New Dog?	Un Nouveau Chien ?
Max's Big Adventure	La Grande Aventure de Max

Why did Emma make Teddy Bear Bread?

"What is that noise?" Max asked Colby.

"I don't know. I've never heard that sound before," said Colby. He was a little worried.

"Meow! Meow!" purred the animal in the tree.

"What is *that*?" both dogs asked each other at the same time.

"I am a cat. My name is Briggs. What is your name?"
"My name is Colby and this is my best friend, Max.
We are..."
"Dogs!" said Briggs in her very I-know-everything voice.

"Welcome to our yard, Briggs!" Max barked. He was very excited to meet someone new.

"We have a special patch of dirt where we love to dig. Come join us," invited Colby.

"This is sooooooooooooooo much fun!" Max barked, as the dirt flew in all directions.
"Jump right in, Briggs. There is plenty of dirt for all of us," barked Colby happily.

"Oh, no thanks. I don't like to get dirty," replied Briggs, in a soft voice. "I prefer to...

claw the bark on a tree," purred Briggs.

"Hmmm ... Clawing a tree doesn't look like much fun to me," said Max to himself.

"What else do you like to do besides clawing the bark on a tree?" asked Colby.

"Well, I *love* to chase butterflies!

Would you like to chase butterflies with me?" Briggs meowed with excitement.

"Ah, no thanks," said Max. "We prefer to chase... hmmm... well, let's see. Colby and I prefer to chase...."

"CATS!" shouted out Briggs.

"YES! That's right! Dogs like to chase cats!" barked Colby. So Max and Colby started chasing after Briggs.

Max and Colby had the best time chasing Briggs around the yellow chairs and behind the swimming pool.

Briggs loved jumping across the woodpile and following Colby under the little tree. They were all having a super fun time running all over the yard.

They raced all around until they were so tired, they had to stop for a rest.

They were happy, and *very* thirsty.

Most of all, they were friends!

"Max and Colby, do you think there is *something* that *both* cats and dogs like to do?" asked Briggs.

Suddenly, they all shouted, "NAPS!
We love to take naps!"

"Max and I always take a nap under the big tree. Let's take a nap together," invited Colby.

"Perrrfect idea!" meowed Briggs, leading the way.

So, Max, Colby, AND Briggs lay down in the shade of the big tree, and took a delightful nap together.

Until...

"Colby, wake up! Where did Briggs go?" Max asked, a bit concerned.

Colby woke up and looked all round. "I don't see her. Why did she leave?" Colby said sadly.

"Look up, Colby. There's Briggs!" whispered Max.

"Briggs is UP in *OUR* tree!" said Colby, thrilled to see the cat.

"Where are you going, Briggs?" asked Max, wanting their new friend to stay and play.

"It's getting late and I am hungry for my dinner. It's time for me to go home," said Briggs, as she was about to jump over the fence.

"Will you come back and play again?" asked Colby.

"Yes, but next time *I will chase you* around the yard!" meowed Briggs, with a smile. And then, she left.

Max and Colby were still a bit tired.

So they curled up side by side, and continued their nap under the big tree.

Draw a picture of Briggs chasing Max and Colby around the yard.

Draw a picture of Briggs, Max and Colby doing an activity that is <u>not</u> in the story.

Acknowledgments

I would like to thank each of the wonderful members of my family and friends who assisted me in writing this story. I so appreciated their excellent suggestions and their constant support.

Family: My husband, Barry Hennessey, our three children and their spouses, Evan & Jenn Hennessey, Meg & Chris Scull, Jared & Liz Hennessey, Karen Dieruf, Bill & Jody Dieruf

Teachers: Mary Chamberlain, Jennifer Connelly, Sue Daigneault, Faith Garnett, Renée A. Mercurio, Sr. M. Catherine Mindling, RSM, Linda Pedersen, Lauren Schultz, Ann Marie Staples.

Children's librarians: Debra Cheney, Susan E. Eiche, Laura Horan, Linda Smart, Susan Williams.

Tech Support Magic: Victor López.

I applaud and deeply thank Teresa Street for putting her heart and soul into illustrating all the "Max & Colby Adventures". Her creative talent puts life into the backyard antics of the two dogs. Teresa and I are a perfect pair because we are the grandmothers of Marcus who knew all the animals in all the stories.

About the Author

Janis Hennessey, along with her husband and three children, have hosted many pets, including dogs, cats, birds, fish, gerbils, rabbits and even snakes, in their New Hampshire home.

At the age of 10 Janis began writing neighborhood plays for her friends in Louisville, Kentucky. Over the years these stories evolved into various children's books. She loves to use the real stories of the family pets and the children in her stories.

Janis earned a master's degree in French Literature from University of Kentucky and a diploma in French History from the Sorbonne, Université de Paris. She taught French in Kentucky, Massachusetts, and New Hampshire where she encouraged her students to write creatively in another language.

About the Illustrator

Teresa Street, a New Hampshire native, is primarily a self-taught artist. She studied with various artists from Texas and New Hampshire as well as took art classes at the University of New Hampshire. She is a past member of the Durham Art Association and has done portrait commission work.

Teresa first met the author 16 years ago when they welcomed their first grandchild. A collaboration ensued to bring Janis' stories to life. The fourth and fifth books add Teresa's family pets into Max and Colby's adventures. Her contribution has been a labor of love for the children, grandchildren and family pets.

THE
END

Made in the USA
Charleston, SC
06 April 2015